Praise for
The Fix-It Friends: Have No Fear!

"Fears are scary! But don't worry: the Fix-It Friends know how to vanquish all kinds of fears, with humor and step-by-step help. Nicole C. Kear has written a funny and helpful series."

—Fran Manushkin, author of the Katie Woo series

"Full of heart and more than a little spunk, this book teaches kids that fear stands no chance against friendship and courage. Where were the Fix-It Friends when I was seven years old?"

—Kathleen Lane, author of *The Best Worst Thing*

"I love the Fix-It Friends as a resource to give to the families I work with. The books help kids see their own power to overcome challenges—and they're just plain fun to read."

—Lauren Knickerbocker, PhD, Co-Director, Early Childhood Clinical Service, NYU Child Study Center

The Fix-It Friends
Sticks and Stones

Nicole C. Kear
illustrated by Tracy Dockray

[Imprint]
MAKE YOUR MARK

NEW YORK

[Imprint]
MAKE YOUR MARK

A part of Macmillan Publishing Group, LLC
175 Fifth Avenue, New York, NY 10010

Library of Congress Cataloging-in-Publication Data is available.

Our books may be purchased in bulk for promotional, educational, or business use. Please contact your local bookseller or the Macmillan Corporate and Premium Sales Department at (800) 221-7945 ext. 5442 or by e-mail at MacmillanSpecialMarkets@macmillan.com.

Book design by Ellen Duda
Illustrations by Tracy Dockray
Imprint logo designed by Amanda Spielman

First Edition—2017

ISBN 978-1-250-11576-8 (hardcover)

1 3 5 7 9 10 8 6 4 2

ISBN 978-1-250-08586-3 (paperback)

1 3 5 7 9 10 8 6 4 2

ISBN 978-1-250-08587-0 (ebook)

mackids.com

Hey, it's Ezra here, and I'm going to break it down for you:

If you're thinking about taking this book without asking permission, just don't do it. It's a seriously dumb idea. Look, we're not going to call you names or anything. And I'm not saying we'll do kung fu on you.

But I'm not saying we *won't*.

You read me?

For Giovanni, my beamish boy,

strong and true

With special thanks to

Lauren Knickerbocker, PhD,

from the NYU Child Study Center

Chapter 1

I'm Veronica Conti and I'm seven. I don't mean to brag, but I'm great at fixing things.

Well, I'm not great at fixing *stuff*, like necklaces or computers or precious glass vases that accidentally got knocked off the shelf and shattered into a billion pieces. I'm better at breaking that kind of stuff than fixing it.

But I can fix problems. In fact, I am the president of a problem-solving group. Just read the sign hanging on my bedroom wall.

When my big brother, Jude, saw my sign, he rolled his eyes and said, "First of all, we're not 'professional.' That means people pay us, and they don't."

So I crossed out *professional* and wrote *world-famous* instead.

Was he satisfied? Of course not.

"'World-famous' isn't true, either," he said. "And you can't say that no problem is too big. What if someone's appendix bursts? That problem would be too big."

Sticks and Stones

"JUDE!" I hollered. "You are driving me bonkers!" I crossed out a bunch of things and wrote new things.

"And you're not the president," he said. "We don't have a president."

Jude is very bossy. He's in fourth grade, and I'm in second, so he is only two years older than me, but he acts like he's already a grown-up.

"Here," I said, taping the sign back up. This is what it said:

THE FIX-IT FRIENDS

Pretty Good
~~Professional~~

Problem Solvers

Most
~~No~~ problems ~~is~~ are
not too BIG!

* Veronica Conti is the president

** Jude Conti's middle name
is B.... BOSSY PANTS!

"Fine," Jude said.

He didn't care that I called him Bossy Pants, because his real middle name is much, much worse than that. It's so embarrassing, he made me swear never to tell a living soul. Or a dead soul, either.

There are four Fix-It Friends. We each made our own personal posters, which I hung up next to the group poster. Jude said he didn't want so many posters cluttering up his bedroom wall, but I said it was *my* wall, actually. We share a bedroom, and we share the walls, too. Two for me, two for him.

My walls are completely full of posters and pictures and fascinating stuff like that. Jude's walls are completely blank because he is completely boring.

These are the posters each of us made. First, Jude's, in his oh-so-perfect penmanship:

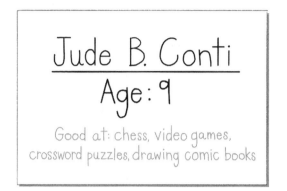

His best friend, Ezra, made a cool sign on his computer:

He didn't write that he was good at speed talking, but he is. In fact, it's the only way he talks. When he grows up, if he is not a rich and famous computer inventor, he could get a job being the person who talks really fast at the end of commercials and says stuff like "No substitutions, exchanges, or refunds. Must be eighteen or older to order."

Cora, who is my best friend, wrote her sign in script. We didn't learn it at school yet, but she taught it to herself:

Cora Klein
☆ Age: 7 ☆
Good at: schoolwork, homework, fashion, mediation, and meditation

I know it seems like she wrote the same word twice, but she didn't. *Mediation* is when you help people stop fighting. It's like being a peacemaker.

Sticks and Stones

Once a week, Cora is a mediator at the recess playground, and so is Jude. I tried to be one, but the mean recess teacher, Miss Tibbs, didn't pick me. She said I had "too much personality" for the job— which doesn't even make sense! That's like saying you can have too much whipped cream. Impossible!

Meditation is totally different and a lot more boring, if you ask me. I tried to meditate once, when our teacher Miss Mabel made us. We folded our legs into lotus position, which is like crisscross applesauce only more uncomfortable. Then we closed our eyes.

"What do we do now?" I asked Miss Mabel.

"We do nothing," she whispered. "We think nothing. We *say nothing.*"

Right away, my nose got soooooo itchy, and I tried to scratch it with my tongue. All the kids laughed, and I got in trouble. But Cora sat perfectly still for so long, if a pigeon had been passing by, he would have thought she was a statue and pooped on her. So it's true. She really is good at meditation *and* mediation.

I made a poster, too. I used turquoise glitter. Everything's better with turquoise glitter.

Veronica Laverne Conti
(President)
Age: 7½
Good at: singing, tag, cartwheels, doing accents, dog training and grooming, talking to people, talking to animals, and just talking, talking, talking

Dad calls me a chatterbox. Mom says I've got the gift of gab. Jude says I'm a motormouth. But

Sticks and Stones

I don't care, because talking is how I find people with problems that need solving.

Like Noah.

I've been friends with Noah since first grade. For a long time, I thought he was mute. That's what you call it when someone doesn't talk. Like when you hit the "mute" button on the TV, and it makes the sound turn off.

I didn't mind that Noah was mute, because you don't have to talk to play tag, and Noah is the best tag player in the universe. He runs so fast, he is basically a blur. One second he's standing in front of you, and the next second he's halfway across the playground.

If I were Noah, I would always be yelling, "Eat my dust!" but he never yells that because he never yells at all.

The Fix-It Friends

I used to think Noah couldn't talk, so I helped him by answering questions for him. Then one day our friend Minnie was giving out Life Savers at recess. She gave one to Noah, but he shook his head. So I explained, "He's allergic."

Then, all of a sudden, Noah opened his mouth, and words came out!

"No, I'm not," he said. "I just don't like the cherry kind. Do you have any pineapple?"

I gasped.

I love to gasp. It adds drama to the day.

"Noah! It's a miracle! You can talk!" I shouted.

"I could always talk," he said.

"You could?"

"Sure," he said oh-so-casually. "I just don't always have something to say."

So Noah's not mute. He's just the quiet type. I always liked that about him.

I always liked it until J.J. Taylor happened. After I saw what J.J. did in the school yard, I started to think that Noah needed to speak up. And if he wouldn't, then the Fix-It Friends would speak up for him.

Chapter 2

At first, I thought Noah and J.J. Taylor were friends because I saw them talking at lunch. I don't sit near Noah at lunch, because he's not in my class and we have to sit at a table with our class. But I see him sometimes, and I always wave. He *always* waves back.

One day in the beginning of November, I was chatting with Minnie and eating my lunch when I spilled my milk all over Minnie's sandwich. I got up to grab some napkins so I could clean up the mess before Miss Tibbs yelled at me. That's when I passed by Noah's table.

I waved like I always do. This time, though, Noah didn't wave back. He was too busy listening to a boy sitting behind him, at the next table.

Here's what the boy looked like:

    1. Tall. Really tall. I could tell even though he was sitting down because his head was so much higher than Noah's head.

    2. Hair that reached down to his

shoulders. It was strawberry blond, which means a bit red and a bit blond. I wish my hair was strawberry blond, but it's just regular lemon blond.

3. Wearing an orange hoodie that was so bright, you could probably see it from outer space. It said FLORIDA on the back.

The mystery boy was sitting at the table next to Noah's. He was leaning way over to talk to him. I do this all the time with Maya, who sits at the table next to mine. Maya sits with her back facing my back, and all I have to do is turn around and leeeeean over. Then I can chat with her or play with her super-long hair or tell her jokes. Once I leaned over a little too far, and I fell backward off the bench. I got a knot on my head, and I got scolded by Miss Tibbs.

The mystery boy was leaning way over to talk to Noah, and the boy was laughing his head off, which is why I thought they were friends. Noah wasn't laughing or talking. But like I said, Noah's kind of mysterious. So I didn't think about it too much.

A few days later at lunch, I got up to get a spork for my mac 'n' cheese. I love sporks! When you need a fork but you also need a spoon, it's just the thing for you. I also love the name. If I ever get a dog, which I probably won't because my dad is allergic, I really, really want to name him Spork.

When I got my spork, I passed Noah. The same mystery boy in the same orange hoodie was leaning over to talk to him. But this time, Noah had his back to the boy, like he wasn't listening.

"Hi, Noah!" I said, but he didn't look up.

"Hey, Noah! Over here!" I said louder. He still didn't look up. He ate his sandwich and chewed very slowly like it was hard work and he had to concentrate on it.

"Noah! Noah Rocha!" I yelled. I said his whole name in case he thought I was talking to another Noah.

The mystery boy looked at me and laughed even harder. Noah looked up, too, and waved, but he didn't smile. In fact, he sort of frowned.

"Noah looks kind of upset," I told Minnie and Cora when I sat back down at our table. "Do you know why?"

Minnie shrugged. "It's hard to know-a with Noah." We both giggled.

Sticks and Stones

Cora said, "Maybe he doesn't like his lunch. That's what's wrong with me. Look what my mom packed for me today!"

Cora slid her lunch box over to show us what was inside—a jar of extra crunchy peanut butter and a cold, cooked corn on the cob.

Cora's mom sometimes puts super-strange things in her lunch box. That's because she's very busy since she has four kids. Cora has an identical twin sister named Camille, and they have two younger brothers, who are also identical

twins. Their names are Bo and Lou, and they're five years old.

When you go to Cora's house, it is always very loud because Bo and Lou like to shout and do karate and battle with foam swords. Cora's mom is always drinking coffee and doing things very fast. She even gets dressed fast. I can tell because lots of times her clothes are on inside out or buttoned up crooked. Usually, she doesn't notice until I tell her. Then she laughs and says, "What would I do without you, V?" She's so busy, she doesn't even have time to say my whole name!

Some mornings, Cora's mom doesn't have time to make lunch, so she just tosses different foods into Cora's lunch box. Minnie calls this "Loco Lunch Box." I tell Cora just to get school lunch on those days, and she refuses because she is a very picky eater. But her lunch problems are easy for me to fix since I like all sorts of food, except broccoli . . . and cauliflower . . . and arugula . . . but Cora's mom never gives her that stuff. So, I just give her some of my lunch and I eat some of hers, and—presto!—problem solved.

So, that's what I did that day at lunch, and soon I forgot all about Noah and how he was upset.

I forgot all about Noah until a few days later, after school, in the yard. That's when I met J.J.

Chapter 3

The yard in back of our school is where we have recess and also get dismissed. It has a climbing wall and a whole jungle gym with monkey bars and slides and firefighter poles and stuff.

It also has a big open place for playing ball and tag and running in circles like a chicken with no head. At dismissal time, all the teachers lead their classes in two lines into that big open space in the yard.

The kids who go to after-school meet by the red doors and go to the gym to do activities. Minnie goes to after-school and says it's really fun. She has learned sewing, yoga, hockey, tap dancing, and

ventriloquism. That's where you hold a dummy and pretend the dummy's talking, but it's really you talking, only you hardly move your lips.

At after-school, you can also learn how to play the piano and speak Spanish, but Minnie already knows how to do that stuff. She even taught me some Spanish, like how to say "*¿Dónde está el baño?*" which means, "Where's the bathroom?" and "*¡Cuidado! ¡No se pare en esa caca del dragón!*" which means, "Watch out! Don't step in that dragon poop!"

The Fix-It Friends

The kids who don't go to after-school get picked up in the yard by their parents or grandparents or babysitters or whoever is in charge of them. A few kids go home in the car or bus, but most everyone lives close to the school, so they can walk home. Some of the fifth graders even get to walk home by themselves! Jude has been begging Mom to let him walk by himself, but Mom says not yet.

Sticks and Stones

If the weather is nice, I always ask Mom or Dad or Nana if we can please, please, please play in the yard for a few minutes before we go home. Lots of other kids do the same thing. After all, who wants to go straight home and do—blegh!—homework? Playing in the yard after school is even more fun than recess. That's because cranky Miss Tibbs isn't there watching us like a hawk.

After school, all the grown-ups are there

standing by the fence, and they watch us. But they are usually busy chatting about boring stuff like the price of college and how broccoli is really good for you. While they are all busy chatting, we can do stuff we're not really allowed to at school recess, like jump off the top of the monkey bars and go headfirst down the slide holding on to one another's ankles.

I always thought it was a good thing that the grown-ups don't pay such close attention to what's happening in the yard. But when the trouble started with J.J. Taylor, I wasn't so sure about that anymore.

It was a Monday, and I was going to Cora's house to play after school. Her mom picked us up. She was holding a jumbo cup of coffee, and her sweater was on backward. She said we could stay in the yard for a while.

Sticks and Stones

Cora's mom always lets her kids play in the school yard, except on the days when they have to go straight to Hebrew school. She wants Bo and Lou to "burn off energy" so they'll be too tired for mischief later at home. Their favorite thing to do is climb on top of the high furniture in their house and wait up there for someone to pass by. Then they yell, "BOO!" and throw stuffed animals at your head.

So when Cora's mom picked us up from school, she said, "Run wild, you monkeys. Run, run, run, run!" I told her that her sweater was on backward, and she laughed and said, "V, you're a lifesaver." Then she zipped her jacket all the way up over the sweater and took a big gulp of her coffee.

"Are you thinking what I'm thinking?" I asked Cora and Camille.

"Zombie Tag!" we all shrieked together. It is funny to hear them talk at the same time because Cora has a squeaky voice like a parakeet, and Camille has a raspy voice like a grizzly bear.

"Let's find Noah!" I said. "He must be here, waiting for Ivy."

Ivy is Noah's babysitter. Listen to this: She is a teenager!

I think teenagers are very fascinating. It's like they are half kid and half grown-up. Sort of like how a centaur is half man and half horse.

Of all the teenagers I've ever met, Ivy is the most interesting. She has four earrings in each ear and one in her nose. I asked her if it hurt, and she said, "Nah. I'm a tough cookie."

She always wears the same black boots, even in the summertime. Guess what's hidden inside the toe part of her boots? Metal! I know that because one time she told me to step on her foot as hard as I could. So I jumped with both feet on her toe, and she didn't even make a peep.

"Steel-toe boots," she said oh-so-casually.

"Wow," I said. "It's like you're wearing a suit of armor on your feet!"

Ivy has super-shiny hair that is as black as midnight except for one chunk in the front. You will never believe what color *that* is. Green!

I ask her a billion questions about her hair.

"How did you make it green?"

"Did it hurt?"

"Will it last forever?"

"Do you use green shampoo?"

She just laughs, which is what she usually does when I ask her questions. Which I do all the time, of course, because she's fascinating!

Ivy has to walk from her school to our school to pick up Noah, so she is usually a few minutes late. That means Noah is always hanging around the yard for a few minutes after school, so he can always play tag.

Most days, Noah runs right over to us, but on this day, he didn't. So we went looking for him. Camille went inside the school to see if he was in the bathroom or at the water fountain. Cora and I walked around the playground. We couldn't find him. Then we saw Matthew Sawyer, who was trying to see how far he could spit. It is one of his favorite hobbies.

The more disgusting something is, the more Matthew Sawyer loves it. His mom is a doctor, so she tells him all about gross things like blood-sucking ticks and flesh-eating bacteria. Then he grosses everyone out by telling us all about it at lunch.

I try to stay away from Matthew Sawyer, but Cora doesn't mind him because Cora doesn't mind anyone. She ran right up to him and said, "Have you seen Noah?"

"Noelle?" he asked, pretending he hadn't heard her. "Nope, haven't seen her."

"Not Noelle! Noah!" I said very loudly.

"Norma?" he said. "I don't think I know a Norma. Is Norma a nit? I think I saw one hatching on your head. You should check there." Then he spat a huge glob of spit way out in front of him and turned to us with a big smile on his face.

I glared at him and walked away. Just when you think Matthew Sawyer can't possibly get more annoying, he does.

"Oh, there's Noah!" squeaked Cora. She pointed to the corner of the school yard, near the climbing wall. Sure enough, there was Noah. He was talking to that mystery boy in the orange hoodie again . . . and he did not look happy.

Chapter 4

The boy was patting the top of Noah's head like Noah was a cutie patootie baby doll or something. He was laughing hard.

Noah wasn't laughing at all. In fact, he was the opposite of laughing. His mouth was all puckered up like he'd just eaten a lemon.

I was wondering why Noah looked so upset. Then I heard what the boy said to Noah. He called him Shorty.

Noah is really short. He's the shortest kid in the second grade.

Personally, I think there are a lot of great things about being short.

1. You can fit in the best hiding places, like under the sink or in a suitcase.

2. You can ride Great Danes, which are my second-favorite dog breed.

3. You are closer to the ground, so when you have to pick up stuff you've dropped, it's easier.

Sticks and Stones

But I don't know any of that for sure, because I'm not short and I'm not tall. I'm just in between. What I do know for sure is that Noah really, really, really hates it when anyone mentions that he's short. He's *sensitive* about it, as my mom would say.

Noah got furious when the boy called him Shorty and patted his head. His eyebrows were all scrunched together, and his face was red.

"Awww, come on, Shorty! It's just a joke!" said the boy.

"Cut it out!" I shouted as Cora and I ran over to them. "Leave Noah alone!"

Noah was surprised to see us. So was the other boy.

"Who are *you*?" the boy asked.

"I'm Cora and this is Veronica. Pleased to meet you!" squeaked Cora. She was acting like she was meeting the queen of England!

The Fix-It Friends

"This is no time for manners!" I whispered to Cora. Then I turned to J.J. and gave him my best Tough Guy Face. Dad taught it to me. He said that Nonno, who is his dad, taught it to him when he was a kid.

Here's how you do it:

    1. Grit your teeth.

    2. Flare your nostrils.

    3. Narrow your eyes and stare really hard.

I have a *very* good Tough Guy Face. Jude's is

terrible. His Tough Guy Face looks more like an On-the-Toilet Face.

So I put on my Tough Guy Face, and I asked the mystery boy, "Who are *you*?"

"I'm J.J. Taylor," he said. "Are you any good at soccer? If you are, you can play with Shorty and me."

"I'm not playing," said Noah.

"Stop calling him Shorty!" I demanded.

I gave J.J. my best stare. And at that exact moment, Jude opened his big mouth and made a lot of trouble for me.

"RONNY!" Jude yelled from across the yard. "Cora's mom wants me to tell you that you guys are leaving in five minutes!"

Ooooh, I was so angry at Jude! If I had been a beekeeper with a swarm of angry bees, I would have definitely let them loose on him.

Jude started calling me Ronny when I was born because he was a toddler and couldn't talk properly. That part isn't his fault. But I have told him and told him that I do not want to be called Ronny anymore! When I was a baby and I couldn't say his name properly, I called him Doody, and you don't see me calling him Doody anymore, do you?

"Your name's Ronny?" J.J. asked me.

"No, it's Veronica," I said, but he just ignored me.

"Ronny's my uncle's name. My big, sweaty, hairy uncle." The more he talked, the louder his voice got.

My blood started to boil. That's really how it feels when I get furious: like I am inside a pot on the stove, getting all heated up.

"My uncle Ronny wears dirty jeans like yours,

too," said J.J., pointing at my legs. "You guys are twins!"

I was so shocked that I didn't know what to say. That almost never happens to me. So I just gasped, and then Cora gasped, and then Noah gasped, too.

Then good old Cora piped up: "That's not a very nice thing to say! Her jeans aren't dirty!"

Here's the thing: Cora was wrong. My jeans *were* dirty. My jeans are usually dirty, and the reason is, I wear them almost every day. And the reason for that is, they are the most comfy pants in the world.

You know how Goldilocks had to eat the burning-hot porridge and the gross cold porridge before she found the one that was absolutely perfect? Well, it is the same with my jeans. Other jeans are too tight or too loose, but these are juuuuust right.

When J.J. said that about my favorite jeans, at first, I was just so surprised. But then my cheeks got burning hot, and I felt super embarrassed. Like I was wearing a pair of grandpa underpants on my head.

I was so embarrassed, I took off running.

Chapter 5

I ran all the way across the yard until I got to the monkey bars, and I climbed up to the very top and sat there. I pulled my handy pack of cinnamon gum out of my jeans pocket.

I always keep some cinnamon gum in there because it cheers me up when I'm feeling down. If I could, I would keep a can of whipped cream in my pocket, but that's too messy, so I bring gum instead.

After a minute, Noah climbed up and sat next to me. I handed him a stick of gum, and he popped it in his mouth.

"How do you know that awful J.J. Taylor?" I asked. "Is he in your class?"

"No, but he was on my soccer team last year," said Noah, chomping on his gum. "He was pretty nice to me then. He told me a lot of stories about his big brother, who's ten years older than him. He went to college in Florida."

"So *that's* why he's wearing that orange hoodie," I said. I smacked my gum. Mom says it's a bad habit and very impolite, but how else can you get the flavor out of the gum, I ask you?

"I wish J.J. would go to Florida and stay there," I grumbled.

"Yeah, me, too," Noah said.

I remembered how Noah hadn't waved at me at lunch, and I said, "Is he teasing you at lunch, too?"

"He was," said Noah with a smile. "But I noticed he ate peanut butter every day, so I told Miss Tibbs I was allergic to peanut butter. She moved my seat so it's far away from him."

"Noah Rocha!" I said. "You are one crafty guy. You aren't allergic to peanut butter!"

"No." He smiled. "But I am allergic to J.J."

Noah hooked his knees on the monkey bars and swung down so he was hanging upside down. I did it, too.

"He's always making dumb jokes about how I'm short," said Noah.

"Did you tell your mom or dad?" I asked. I've never met his parents, but I know his dad is kind of famous. He used to be a soccer star in Brazil. Now he has his own radio show called *The Rafael Rocha Radio Hour*. My dad listens to it sometimes, and once I listened with him. I thought Noah's dad would do something interesting like sing songs or tell jokes or say stuff about Noah. But all he did was talk about soccer. It was pretty boring.

"I don't want to tell my parents," Noah said. "It's embarrassing."

"What about Ivy?"

He shook his head.

I grabbed the bar and pulled my legs off so I was standing right next to Noah, who was still upside down.

Sticks and Stones

"Noah! You have to tell Ivy!"

"Tell me what?"

We had been so busy chatting, we didn't notice Ivy walk over. She was wearing hoop earrings that were so big, they almost touched her shoulders!

Noah swung off the monkey bars.

"I have to tell you I'm really hungry," he said. "Can we get a slice of pizza?"

"Sure," said Ivy.

"Ivy, have you ever gotten a guinea pig to jump through your earrings?" I asked. "They are the perfect size!"

I was being serious, but she just laughed. Then she and Noah left, and Cora came to tell me that we had to go, too.

Chapter 6

Cora lives one block away from the school, on top of a bakery. It's not her family's bakery, though, so she doesn't get to eat as many free cupcakes as she wants, which is too bad. But it's still nice that she lives there because her house always smells sweet, like chocolate-chip cookies fresh out of the oven.

As we walked from the school to Cora's house, I asked her if I could borrow something to wear.

"I think I got mud on my pants," I said.

She looked down at me and said, "No, you didn't."

Then her eyes got big. "You just want to change those pants because J.J. teased you!"

Sticks and Stones

"That's not why!" I exclaimed. Even though it really was. "I just feel like a change!"

Cora tilted her head and looked at me for a few seconds.

"Okay," Cora agreed. Then she suddenly smiled really big and clapped her hands. "Oooooh! I can give you a MAKEOVER!"

"Oh no. Not another makeover," groaned Camille, who was walking next to us. "She gave me one last week, and she tried to make my curls straight. Know how she did it?"

I shook my head.

"She tied rocks to the end of my hair," said Camille. "My head was so heavy, I got a huge pain in my neck!"

All the Klein twins have the same super-curly red hair, which is something I have always wanted. Every year when I blow out my birthday

candles, I wish my hair would turn curly. First of all, it would look sensational. Second of all, curly hair is so fluffy, it must be like walking around with a pillow attached to your head, which is very convenient.

"You're bonkers!" I said to Cora. "Why would you ever want to make hair *un*-curly, for crying out loud?"

"I thought she would look more glamorous that way," said Cora.

Camille just rolled her eyes. She is not the glamorous type. Her hair is always messy and has so many twigs and leaves in it, I wouldn't be surprised if a bird made a nest in there one day. That would be the coolest thing ever. Then she could sneak a pet into school.

"Anyway, Veronica doesn't need a makeover," said Camille. "She shouldn't change just 'cause some kid said something dumb."

"But makeovers are so fun!!!" squealed Cora.

"If I were you, I'd run for my life," said Camille. "Her makeovers are deadly."

"Take over the makeover! Take over the makeover!" chanted Bo and Lou. They love battles and showdowns and surprise attacks.

We walked past the bakery, which smelled like cinnamon and apples, and into Cora's apartment. Cora took me right into the bedroom she shares with Camille. She flung open the closet doors.

You could tell which clothes were Cora's because they were all skirts and dresses, and they were full of polka dots. Everything was very clean, and her clothes hung neatly from the hangers.

Camille's side of the closet looked more like my closet, with most of the clothes piled up in a big heap on the floor.

Cora looked at one dress and then another and then another, and she kept frowning and sighing and saying, "Hmmm."

Then she squealed.

"This is it!" she said, pulling out a dress and holding it up high so I could get a good look.

Here is what the dress looked like:

1. Bright bubble gum pink. With black polka dots.

2. Poofy. The skirt part had all this crinkly scratchy stuff underneath to make it poof up like a princess ball gown.

3. With a black lacy collar and a shiny black belt. "It's patent leather," said Cora, even though I didn't have any idea what that meant.

Here are three things I hate to have on my clothes:

1. Scratchy stuff.

2. Collars.

3. Belts.

It was my worst nightmare of a dress. I could almost hear horror movie music playing in my head when she showed it to me.

But Cora looked so happy. She was beaming.

So I put it on. It was worse than I thought it would be. The scratchy stuff felt like an army of spiders itching my legs. The collar felt like it was choking me. And the pink was so bright, I felt like I needed sunglasses to even look at it. I didn't think it could get worse. Then Cora buckled the belt.

"This dress is trying to kill me," I gasped.

Cora giggled. She spun me around so she could look at me.

"Oh, Veronica!" she whispered. "You look absolutely . . ."

"Ridiculous?" I said.

"Perfect!" she said. "You have to wear this to school tomorrow!"

Then, all of a sudden, we heard this enormous roar from above our heads. And sure enough, there on top of the bookshelf were Bo and Lou.

"TAKE OVER THE MAKEOVER!!!!!" they hollered.

Before we knew it, stuffed animals were flying at our heads.

"Ahhh!!" we screamed, and we ran out of the room.

Chapter 7

I brought Cora's dress—or as I liked to call it, Monster Dress—home in my backpack. The next morning, instead of putting on my favorite jeans like I always did, I put it on.

When I walked into the kitchen for breakfast, Dad was so shocked, he spilled his coffee all over his shirt.

Then Mom came in. When she saw me, she made a surprised squeak that sounded just like Ezra's guinea pig, Ziggy.

"Wow!" she said. Then she said it again. "Wow!"

Then Jude walked in, reading one of his spooky

books. This one was called *Revenge of the Zom-bunny.*

Jude reads while he walks all the time, which he is not allowed to do, because it makes him bump into stuff. Once he was reading while walking through the supermarket and bumped into a huge pyramid of Granny Smith apples. It started an apple avalanche!

So he walked into the kitchen with his nose in the book, and, of course, he bumped into the refrigerator. That made him look up.

Guess what he did when he saw me in Monster Dress? What's the meanest, worst thing a big brother could do? Yep, he burst out laughing.

"Is it Halloween?" he said.

"MOM!" I yelled.

"Jude," she scolded.

"I was only joking!" he said.

"Well, it wasn't funny!" I replied. "There's plenty I could tease you about, you know. Like your eyeglasses. How would *you* like it if I called you Four-Eyes? Or a geek?"

"Geek is chic," said Jude.

"Or I could make fun of your dumb books about mutant vegetables and vampire goldfish. They're weird! You're a weirdo!"

"Veronica," Mom said, and she gave me her *Cut it out* look.

"It's okay," Jude said oh-so-calmly. "Thanks for the compliment."

Nothing makes me more angry than when Jude doesn't get angry when I am trying to bother him.

"Jude!" I yelled. "You're driving me crazy!"

Dad laughed and said, "Jude has a great poker face, huh?"

"He *does* have a great face for poking," I grumbled. "That's what I'd like to do right now."

"It means I don't show how I'm feeling," Jude the know-it-all said. "It's what you're supposed to do when you play poker so no one can guess what cards you have."

"And it works like a charm when someone's teasing you," said Dad. "Drives 'em nuts."

I scowled, which is the opposite of a poker face. Jude laughed but in a nice way.

"I'm sorry for teasing you, Ronny Bo-Bonny,"

he said, calling me by the nickname that always makes me smile. "You just look different, that's all."

"Well, I think you look fabulous," Mom said, "and besides, variety is the spice of life!" My mom is very cheerful. That's kind of surprising because her job is to listen to people talk about their problems all day long. She is a therapist, and she has an office on the bottom floor of our building.

She has these machines plugged in down there that make a ton of noise, just so you can't hear what people are saying through the door. But I can still hear when people yell and when they cry loudly. Sometimes I even hear people laughing, and then I have to scold Mom and tell her to stop goofing off at work.

"Want a fancy hairstyle to go with your fancy dress?" Mom asked. "French braids?"

I nodded.

Sticks and Stones

Just then, I heard footsteps in the hall.

"PWETTY!" squealed a little voice from the kitchen doorway. And who should run in but Pearl!

Pearl's the cutest two-year-old in the universe. Especially when she wakes up and her short blond hair sticks up in all directions like a cartoon character who got zapped by lightning.

In the morning, Pearl always has her two favorite things with her: Chooch and Ricardo. Chooch is her pacifier. I named it that because Nana and Nonno, who come from Italy, say that the Italian word for pacifier is *ciuccio*, which you say like this: "choo-cho."

Ricardo is a big black rat. He's stuffed, of course. Pearl absolutely loves rats. They are her favorite animal. Pearl has had Ricardo for so long and played with him so much that his tail fell off. So

Dad stuck it back on with silver duct tape. Now Jude calls him Franken-Rat.

Pearl liked my Monster Dress so much, she wanted to wear her fancy party dress to day care. It was blue with little flowers all over the front and lace on the bottom. It was also too small for her, so when she put it on, you could see her diaper underneath.

Then she asked Mom to draw whiskers on her face so she would look like a rat. Mom used

her black eyeliner and drew three straight whiskers on each cheek.

"Pwetty wat pwincess!" Pearl said when she looked in the mirror. You could tell she felt fabulous in her dress. Too bad I didn't feel that way in mine.

Chapter 8

Monster Dress itched me and choked me all day at school, but lots of people said nice things about it.

Miss Mabel said, "Veronica! You look absolutely faboo!" That meant a lot because not only is she my favorite teacher of all time, but she also has the best outfits of any grown-up I have ever met.

Miss Tibbs said, "Miss Conti, the dress suits you nicely."

And Minnie spun me around and said, "*Linda!*"

I said, "I didn't change my name, for crying out loud."

"No," she laughed. "It means 'pretty' in Spanish."

Then I said, "*¡Cuidado! ¡No se pare en esa caca del dragón!*" and we laughed because dragon poop is just plain funny.

Not everyone was nice, of course.

"If you ask me," said Matthew Sawyer, "you look like an enormous bubble gum bubble with black ants stuck on you. I can almost hear them screaming, 'Help! Freeeeeee us!'"

"Well, good thing I *didn't* ask you!" I said.

After school, Dad picked up me and Jude—and Cora and Ezra, too. He let us play in the yard like he always does, but he said we could only play for a few minutes because a problem had come up at his job and he had to take care of it.

My dad's a super, which means he fixes stuff that breaks in people's apartments. He works in a tall building near our school called the Monroe. When he goes to work, he has to carry a jumbo key ring that has about a hundred keys on it. If there are old keys that don't work anymore, he gives them to me. Now I have a whole collection of my own. You never know what locks they might open!

On the days when Dad picks us up, he is usually all done with his super work for the day. But every so often, there are emergencies in the Monroe and he has to stop by and take a look. Once, someone's refrigerator door fell off. Another time, a whole bunch of crickets that were supposed to be food for a bearded dragon escaped. They were jumping all over the tenth floor and chirping like crazy!

"What's the emergency this time, Dad?" I asked him. "Can we come?"

"Yeah, you guys can tag along if you promise to stay out of trouble," Dad said. "It's just Mr. Luntzgarten's heater again. He says it's making a racket."

The Fix-It Friends

Mr. Luntzgarten is the Grinch-iest, grouch-iest grump in the Monroe. He also has the biggest eyebrows of any human being I have ever seen. Maybe they itch him and that's what makes him so cranky. He is always complaining about every-thing, including:

1. The elevator beeping too loud.
2. His doorbell ringing too loud.
3. His neighbor's dog barking too loud.
4. Me being too loud.

"Hey, we can hang out at my apartment while you fix the heater," said Ezra. "I'll go ask my mom for the key."

One of the best parts of the Monroe is that Ezra lives there with his mom, who is the princi-pal of our school. Principal Powell is really nice. She has a sign in her office that says, NOBODY'S

Sticks and Stones

PERFECT. THAT'S WHY PENCILS HAVE ERASERS. I know
that because I have been sent to her office a few
times, but all the times were because of accidents.

Dad said okay, so Ezra and Jude ran to get the
key from Principal Powell. Cora and I went to get
Noah so we could play tag for a few minutes.

I was a little nervous about running into J.J.
again, but at least he couldn't make fun of my dirty
jeans anymore, because I was wearing Monster
Dress. And besides, Noah might need our help.

Cora spotted Noah by the climbing wall. Right
next to him was J.J. Taylor. Noah was turned away
from him, looking down at the ground, and J.J.
was tapping his shoulder.

"Come on, Shorty!" J.J. was saying. "It'll be fun!"

"Why don't you pick on somebody your own
size?" I shouted as I ran over.

J.J. looked confused for a few seconds, like he

didn't recognize us. Then he said, "Is that you,

Uncle Ronny?"

"It's VERONICA!" I hollered.

I got so mad, so fast. I was about to put on my

Tough Guy Face, but then I remembered Jude's

poker face and thought I should try that instead.

"What's the matter with you?" Cora whispered

when she saw my face.

Sticks and Stones

"Nothing," I said. "This is my Nothing-Is-the-Matter Face."

"I think it needs some work," she whispered politely. "Right now it seems like your I-Am-Choking-on-a-Fish-Bone Face."

I made my eyebrows go down, and then I made them go up again and I puffed my cheeks out, but I just got so confused, I didn't know what to do with my face.

The whole time, J.J. was looking at me funny.

"You look different," said J.J. "Doesn't she, Shorty?"

Noah glowered at him.

"You don't look like my uncle Ronny anymore," said J.J.

"See?" Cora whispered to me. "The makeover worked!"

"Now you look like Uncle Ronny's baby, Jojo!

She has a big poofy dress just like that," said J.J., laughing.

"I DO NOT look like BABY JOJO!" I yelled. I didn't know what Baby Jojo looked like, but I knew I did not want to look like her.

"Can't you take a joke?" J.J. asked. He was laughing so hard, he was doubled over. His laugh wasn't a little giggle or even a medium-sized chuckle. It was a huge, gigantic guffaw. Miss Mabel taught us that word. She said it's when you're laughing so hard, you are howling and slapping your knees. And that's what J.J. was doing—right at me!

I got so mad, I growled, "At least I don't look like a big, juicy Florida orange!"

He stopped laughing and scowled. "Hey, I like Florida."

I was so mad, I felt like a bull staring at a red cape. Noah and Cora noticed that I was about to charge, so they each grabbed one of my arms and led me away.

"What are we going to do?" asked Cora. She was pulling on her corkscrew curls, which is what she does when she's nervous. "He can't just keep teasing you guys!"

"Oh, he won't," I promised. "Noah, ask Ivy if you can come to Ezra's house. We're making a plan. And we're calling backup."

"What does that mean?" asked Noah.

"It means, the Fix-It Friends are on the case!"

Chapter 9

Ivy said Noah could come over, and she offered to watch us while Dad fixed the heater. So all of us walked together to the Monroe, where we had a big meeting at Ezra's apartment.

The first thing I did at Ezra's house was visit Ziggy, Ezra's guinea pig. I am absolutely dying to get a pet, but my dad is allergic to pretty much any animal with fur, especially dogs, which are my favorite. I would settle for a snake, but Mom says they give her the heebie-jeebies. So for now, I have to play with other people's pets. Ziggy is one of my favorites.

He's a real furball. His brown fur is so long that

his face is kind of hidden underneath it all. Ziggy is so smart that when you call his name, he runs right over to you. And he can do tricks!

I asked Ivy if I could borrow one of her big hoop earrings, and guess what? Ziggy jumped right through it!

"That guinea pig is a rock star," said Ivy.

After we played with Ziggy, I asked for iced tea, which Ezra always has in his fridge. Not regular old iced tea but hibiscus tea, which is made from flowers! Ezra says it's what he and his mom drink in Jamaica. He goes there every summer because that's where his mom was born and where his grandma and grandpa live. He says that in Jamaica, the ocean is as warm as a bubble bath and you can catch little lizards and eat coconuts that fall off trees.

Ezra also says you can eat green bananas

there. I saw some at his house once, and I said, "Ummm, Ez? I think you should throw those out. They're completely green." But then he explained that they were special bananas called plantains and they are *supposed* to be green. You learn something new every day, as my dad would say.

After school, I asked Ezra for some hibiscus tea, and also for potato chips. Ivy had a snack

with us, and then she said she had to study for a big chemistry test.

"What's chemistry?" I asked.

"It's a kind of science where you mix chemicals and sometimes blow up stuff," she explained. "It's kind of awesome."

Then she put these enormous headphones on her ears and turned on some super-loud music. I thought it was weird that she could listen to such loud music and study at the same time, but like I said, teenagers are very strange, and Ivy is the strangest one of all.

While Ivy studied in the kitchen, the rest of us went into the living room. Cora and Noah and I acted out the whole story about J.J. Taylor for Jude and Ezra. I am a great actor, so I played J.J. and laughed a lot like a big baboon. Cora played me doing my great Tough Guy Face and awful poker face. Noah played himself, nodding a lot.

When we were done, Jude said, "Noah, you should tell Ivy or your parents."

Noah shook his head.

"Jude's right," said Ezra. "Or you could tell my mom. My mom deals with stuff like this all the time."

Noah shook his head really fast then.

"You could tell J.J.'s mom," said Cora. "Or I could tell her. Grown-ups love me."

"It's true," I agreed. "She puts them under a magic spell of cuteness. They are powerless to resist!"

Cora giggled.

"But his mom isn't there after school," said Noah. "Just his dad. And he's even more scary than J.J. He's ten feet tall. I saw him walk through

Sticks and Stones

the red doors at school once, and he had to bend down so he didn't hit the doorway."

"That doesn't mean he's mean," I pointed out. "My dad's tall, and he's an old softy."

But Noah just shook his head.

"Let me help you talk to J.J.," said Jude. Just because he's been a recess mediator for a few years, he thinks he can always save the day.

"It won't work," said Noah. "I'll just ignore him."

"Yeah, that's what I did with Gary Grotowski last year," said Ezra, cracking his knuckles. "He kept saying stupid stuff about my braces and calling me Metal Mouth—"

I couldn't help interrupting him: "Why would he tease you about braces? They are so cool! I can't wait to get some. Then I'll be half robot."

"Oh, people can tease you about *anything*," said Ezra very fast. "Kids are always getting sent down to my mom's office for teasing, and she says she's heard kids called names for everything. For their clothes or their hair or their voices or their glasses or their grades or whatever. Even for stuff that's great, like being too smart or too pretty or too nice."

"Can a person be too nice?" squeaked Cora. I could tell she was worried.

"No, of course not!" I laughed.

Sticks and Stones

"So last year, Gary Grotowski kept calling me Metal Mouth, and I just had to use my all-star, Grade A poker face. You know what my secret is? I imagined his stupid words bouncing off me like foam balls. Bounce! Bounce! Bounce!"

"Yeah, they're just words," agreed Noah. "It's not like he's hurting me."

Jude was shaking his head. "Sometimes words do hurt you. A poker face is great and all, but sometimes it's not enough."

For once in my life, I totally agreed with him.

"You know what I think?" I said. "I think we should stand up to that J.J. Taylor!"

"Absolutely!" squeaked

Cora. She nodded her head, and her curls bounced like crazy.

"Give him a taste of his own medicine!" I cried.

"Positively!" Cora chirped.

"Do kung fu on him!"

"What?" screeched Cora.

"What?" asked the others.

I jumped up to my feet and did some kicks.

"Kung fu!" I repeated. "We won't actually *attack* him. We'll just show him we know how, and then he'll never bother us again!"

"Ummm, yeah, I get what you're saying, but no, I don't think so," said Ezra.

"That's probably the worst idea I've ever heard," said Jude.

"We don't even know kung fu," said Noah.

So I had to give one of my special speeches.

Sticks and Stones

I am *very* good at speeches that convince people I'm right. Dad says I should be a lawyer.

"Aren't you tired of being teased?" I asked everyone. "Aren't you sick of feeling embarrassed? Well, here's our answer! It's KUNG FU!!!"

Then I raised my fist in the air and hollered, "Who's with me?"

No one was with me—at first. But I kept on giving speeches like that until Jude said, "Okay, okay, okay! If we help a little, will you stop talking?" and I said, "Sure."

Ezra put on a record from his mom's collection, which played a very jazzy tune all about kung fu fighting. Then Ezra found a website about kung fu that showed some super-cool moves. They were all named after animals, like the dragon, the tiger, the snake, the leopard, and the crane.

The Fix-It Friends

The crane kick was the easiest one, so I chose that. Here's how you do it:

1. Put your arms up straight and high, to make a V shape above your head.

2. Stand on one leg, on tiptoe.

3. Bend the other leg and lift it off the ground.

Now, that last part *sounds* easy, but it is not.

Sticks and Stones

I tried it ten times, and every time, I fell. On the last time, not only did I fall, I fell right on top of Ezra's spectacular Lego skyscraper.

"Oh no!" I yelped.

I raised my hands really fast to cover my eyes. When I did that, I heard a loud *riiiiiiip*.

Then I felt coldness on my back.

"Oops," I whispered.

"My dress!" Cora shrieked. "There's a big humongous rip in the back!"

It *had* been feeling a bit tight.

After that, we stopped doing kung fu and started cleaning up one million Legos. I said sorry to Ezra and Cora a hundred times. I told them I'd give them all my allowance. I told them I'd be their servant for life! But they were both really nice about it.

You know who wasn't nice about it? Guess.

"Do you have a magnet inside you that attracts trouble?" asked Jude.

"It was an accident!" I scowled at him. "Both things!"

Then I remembered the sign in Principal Powell's office.

"Nobody's perfect!" I cried. "That's why pencils have erasers."

"Well, your pencil needs an extra big eraser," said Jude. "Maybe even two."

Chapter 10

The next day, I decided to wear my favorite jeans. Mom had washed them, so they were nice and clean. Boy, did it feel great not to have a collar choking me and an army of spiders scratching my legs.

I felt bad about ripping Monster Dress, but Nana said she'd fix it. She used to be a seamstress, and she can sew anything!

"Don' worry-a," she said. "I will-a darn it!"

"Nana," I scolded. "You don't have to curse!"

She laughed and told me that to darn a hole means to sew it up. I love it when one word means two things. Like the word *calf*. If you said, "My calf is killing me!" you could mean that your leg muscle hurts a lot, but you could also mean your baby cow is attacking you. How cool is that?

Sure enough, Nana had Monster Dress all darned and folded in a bag for Cora when she came to pick me up from school.

Nana picks us up sometimes when Mom and Dad are working. My grandpa, Nonno, usually stays home and works in his garden or paints a

picture. He says too many children give him a headache. When he says that, Nana always calls him a "grump-pa," which cracks me up.

I like it when Nana picks us up because she always lets us play in the yard and always brings us sweet treats, like licorice or cookies or gummi bears. Dad says she spoils us rotten, but Nana says that's her job.

Pearl was with Nana because she goes to day care only three days a week, the lucky dog. The other two days, she probably lies on Nana and Nonno's couch gobbling chocolate bars and watching TV while I'm taking spelling tests and adding a million numbers and meditating!

Pearl was still dressed in her Rat Princess outfit. She loved it so much, she had even slept in it! She'd wanted to wear it in the bath, too, but Mom said, "Now, that is where I draw the line," and made her take it off. Pearl was also wearing my old tiara, which was bent and missing most of its rhinestones. And Mom had drawn the three black whiskers on her face again.

"Pearl!" gushed Cora. "You look marvelous! Are you a cat princess?"

Pearl made a disgusted face. She doesn't like cats very much.

"No!" she cried. "A wat!"

"Would the Rat Princess like a gummi bear?" I asked her.

"Wats eat twash," she said very seriously. But then she grabbed the gummi bear out of my hand. "And gummis!!"

After Cora and I had eaten a whole bunch of gummi bears—heads first, of course—we told Nana we had to do something important.

We got Ezra and Jude, and then we all ran

over to where Noah was waiting for Ivy by the climbing wall. J.J. was bothering him, as usual. It was easy to spot them because J.J. was wearing his orange jacket and an orange knit hat, too. I looked around for J.J.'s ten-foot-tall dad, but I didn't see anyone that tall anywhere.

"Aw, come on, Shorty," J.J. was saying. "Just one game of soccer? Please?"

Noah shook his head.

"Wanna play baseball instead?" asked J.J. "Hey, I know! You could play *short*stop! Get it? Get it?"

Then J.J. howled with laughter. That did it!

"Get in formation!" I whispered to the others. We had decided to make a semicircle, but they didn't do such a great job. It looked more like a squiggly worm shape than a semicircle.

"Good afternoon," said Cora. "May we speak with you, please?"

"No manners!" I whispered to her.

J.J. laughed. "Ronny, why do you look so mad?"

"I look mad," I said, "because I am mad. I'm steaming mad. I'm blazing mad." With every word, I walked a little closer to him. Cora, Minnie, Ezra, and Jude shuffled along next to me.

Then I stared at him reeeeeally hard and I said, "And you know what else, J.J. Taylor?"

"What?" he asked. He looked really confused.

"We know KUNG FU!!!!" I shouted. Fast as lightning, I got into the crane pose.

Sticks and Stones

I looked over my shoulder and said, "Go!" Then the other Fix-Its got into their poses, too, but they were pretty halfhearted. Jude didn't look like a dragon at all. He looked like a nervous weasel.

I turned to J.J. and I yelled, "No! More! TEASING!"

Then I did my crane kick. Or, at least, I tried to.

I wasn't going to actually kick J.J. I was just going to kick near him, so he'd be scared and know I meant business. But I was so excited that I kicked too high, and before I knew what was happening, I was slipping and falling forward and landing hard on my knee.

"Ow," I panted. "Ow ow ow ow ow."

I fell so hard that there was a hole in the knee of my favorite jeans. Under the hole, there was a big bloody scrape.

I hate blood. I really, truly hate blood. It makes me feel all dizzy like I am maybe going to faint.

I started to cry.

Jude ran to get Nana. The rest of the kids gathered around to help me—even J.J.

"Oh no! Don't cry," said J.J.

Then, to my amazement, he took off his Florida hoodie and rolled it into a ball, and then he put it under my hurt knee like a pillow.

Nana rushed over and gave me a hug, and then I cried really hard. I didn't even care who saw. It hurt a lot. But I was also crying because I was so disappointed that my plan hadn't worked, and I was mad that my favorite jeans were ripped, and I was confused about J.J.

Pearl started to cry, too. Her tears made her whiskers get all smeared.

"Wonny bwoken!" she cried.

"No, no, *bella*. She's-a not broken. Just-a little-a boo-boo!" said Nana.

"Fix my Wonny!" Pearl demanded. She said it like I was her baby doll or something.

"Want a piece of gum?" J.J. asked me. "When I

get hurt, my brother always gives me gum to make me feel better. Or anyway, he used to."

Then he handed me a stick of wintergreen gum. It's not my favorite, but it's my second favorite.

Weird, weird, weird, I thought. *Weird that J.J. uses gum to cheer up like I do and weird that J.J. is being so nice all of a sudden.*

I didn't know what to think.

Ivy came over, wearing earrings that were the shape of skulls and crossbones in all of her earring holes.

"What happened here?" she asked Noah.

"Umm . . . it's kind of a long story," Noah said.

"That's cool. I've got all the time in the world," said Ivy. I knew that she would make Noah spill the beans now even though he wanted to keep his problem private. That was one thing I could be relieved about, at least.

Chapter 11

When we got home, I sat on the side of the bathtub while Jude cleaned my scrape. He is absolutely the best at that stuff. Here's why:

1. He is very gentle when he cleans the cut.

2. He has his own personal collection of cool Band-Aids. He buys them with his allowance, and sometimes he lets me use them. They have old-fashioned spooks on them like Frankenstein, the bride of Frankenstein, and Dracula.

3. He never, ever uses alcohol to
clean your cut, which is what
Dad uses. Dad thinks it's the
only thing that really works, but
I think it's cruel and unusual
punishment.

Jude patted my knee very gently with a cotton ball full of hydrogen peroxide.

"Remember when you used to call it High Dragon Rocks Hide?" he asked me.

I giggled. "Yeah, I thought they called it that because it was a magical potion they found hiding in the rocks up in the mountain, where dragons fly."

"And then one day you got a scrape and asked Dad to use the High Dragons stuff, and he had no idea what you were talking about," Jude said, smiling.

"And finally, I just had to pull it out of the medicine cabinet and show him—"

"And then he laughed so hard, he cried."

"Yeah, but it wasn't a nasty laugh like J.J.'s," I said. "Because Dad's nice and funny and not mean. He's like you."

Jude smiled. Sometimes I feel like we are enemies, but then other times I feel like we are the best of friends.

"J.J. was pretty nice when you got hurt. Maybe

he's not so bad," Jude pointed out. "Plus I think he misses his big brother."

Jude stuck a Headless Horseman Band-Aid on my knee, very carefully.

"If you went to Florida, I'd probably miss you a little," I said. But really, I was thinking, *I don't know what I'd do! It would be worse than broccoli for breakfast, lunch, and dinner. It would be worse than having chicken pox on my birthday or having to go to school in the summertime!*

"Uggggh," I groaned. "Why doesn't J.J. just make up his mind? Is he nice or nasty? A bully or a buddy?"

"Who's a bully-a?" Nana asked. She had walked in without us even noticing, that sneaky lady.

Jude left and I told Nana everything. When I was done, I felt really relieved. She was quiet for a minute, and then she said, "I'm gonna make-a some tea and tell-a you a story."

Nana and I love to drink tea, especially peppermint. Sometimes if I'm miserable, she lets me drink out of these special cups and saucers that used to belong to her mother. They are super dainty and delicate and have dancing ladies on them.

Since I was miserable *and* bleeding, Nana let me use the special teacups, *and* she gave me a butter cookie to dunk. Nonno came in then and said, "What am I? Chopped liver?" which meant he wanted tea and cookies, too.

"When I was a little girl-a, I was-a very skinny," Nana said.

"It's true! She was like a toothpick!" laughed Nonno. He knows that because they were friends when they were kids.

"There was a girl-a who lived on-a my street. Her name was-a—"

"Isabella Clara Santini!" Nonno interrupted. "And she was crazy about donkeys. I don't know why. She just loved donkeys like you wouldn't believe."

I giggled. I always like hearing stories about when they were kids in Italy. Some stuff was so different then, but other stuff was exactly the same as it is now.

"And-a do you know-a what Isabella Clara Santini called-a me?" asked Nana.

I shook my head.

"*Ranocchia!*" Nana and Nonno said at the same time.

"What's that mean?" I asked, dunking my cookie in my tea.

"It means 'froggy,'" said Nonno. "Because Nana's legs were so skinny, she looked like a frog."

"But that's so mean of Isabella!" I exclaimed. I couldn't believe someone had made fun of my darling nana!

"Yes," said Nana, sipping her tea. "Every-a time she saw-a me, she called me *ranocchia*. I was-a so embarrassed that-a I always wore long-a dresses to cover my-a legs."

"One time we all went to the beach, and your nana stayed in her long dress in the hot sun all day and never went swimming," said Nonno, shaking his head.

"Nana!" I said. "How awful!"

Nana nodded. "Then-a, one day-a, I was playin' ball by-a myself in front-a our house. Isabella was-a walkin' home, holdin' this little clay-a donkey she made at school-a. It was-a very pretty and painted all-a different colors. And-a then, just-a like always, Isabella called me *ranocchia* again!"

"Nana was so mad, she threw the ball right at Isabella," said Nonno, "and it knocked the sculpture out of her hand, and it broke into a million little pieces."

"No!" I gasped. My nana is always proper. She

wears pearls and perfume. I couldn't imagine her ever doing anything so . . . so . . . so naughty!

"And-a Isabella picked-a up the donkey's broken head-a, and she was-a cryin' and cryin'. I said-a I was sorry. Then I asked her-a why she called me *ranocchia*. But-a she just-a shrugged. So I said, 'Well-a, stop-a! It makes me feel-a terrible!'"

"And after that," Nonno said, "Isabella Clara Santini never called her *ranocchia* again."

I gulped down the last of my tea.

"I get it!" I cried. "I should throw a ball at J.J.!"

Nana and Nonno shook their heads.

"I should make him cry?"

More head shaking.

"I should take something he really loves and break it into a billion pieces?" Even more head shaking.

"Talk-a to him. No kung-a fu. No shoutin.' Just-a strong, clear-a words," said Nana.

"Okay." I nodded.

Nana kissed me on the head. Then she said she knew just how to darn my favorite jeans so they would be as good as new—better than new, in fact. She whisked them away with a wink.

The next morning, when I woke up, I saw my jeans hanging on my closet door. Instead of a big, ugly rip in the knee, there was a big fabric star sewed on.

Guess what color it was?

Turquoise!

And guess what it had all over it?

Glitter!

That Nana must be my fairy grandmother! My darn fairy grandmother!

Chapter 12

All day at school, I felt fabulous in my comfy old jeans with the new patch. I felt like nothing could get me down!

At recess, Cora and I asked Noah what Ivy had said when he told her about J.J.

"Well, she said she was going to get J.J. a one-way ticket to a dungeon in Siberia. But then she changed her mind and said that first I should try talking it out, and *then*, if that didn't work, we could try Siberia."

I laughed.

"Ivy made me tell my parents, too," said Noah.

"Ooooh, I bet your dad was furious at J.J.!" I said. "I bet he'll say something mean about him on *The Rafael Rocha Radio Hour!*"

"But it's a sports show," said Cora. "And anyway, he can't just say mean stuff on the radio. He'd get fired."

Cora is always sensible. It's lucky for her she has me as her best friend to add some spice to the day!

Noah nodded. "He was a little mad, and he said some stuff in Portuguese that I didn't really understand. But then he told me the same thing as Ivy. To try talking first."

Sticks and Stones

"I can help you talk to J.J.," squeaked Cora.

"Okay," said Noah.

"Me, too!" I said.

"Ummmm, I don't know." He looked a little nervous.

"Just because I broke Ezra's Legos . . . and Cora's Monster Dress . . . and my own knee does not mean I will mess up the talk!"

"It's just too many people," said Cora. "You know what they say about too many cooks in the kitchen."

"Too many cooks in the kitchen probably make a delicious feast with homemade whipped cream for dessert!" I said in a huff. But then I got a great idea.

"I know!" I hopped up and down. "I'll hide nearby in case you need backup."

"Okay," said Noah, "and we can have a code

word. And if I say the code word, it means 'Come quick!'"

"Yes! Yes! Yes!" I cried.

I *love* code words. My first favorite thing is bulldogs, and my second favorite thing is days off from school, but my third favorite thing is code words.

"How about *tuberculosis*?" I suggested.

"Or *patent leather*?" said Cora.

Sticks and Stones

"Or *¡Cuidado! No se pare en esa caca del dragón?*" I said.

Noah cracked up. Then he said, "What about *hopscotch*?"

"Perfect!" Cora and I agreed.

"Perfect?" asked Matthew Sawyer. He has this annoying habit of just popping his big head right into the middle of a private conversation.

"What's perfect? Are you talking about my face? Or my hair? Or my report card?"

I rolled my eyes. "The only perfect thing about you, Matthew Sawyer, is your pestiness. You're a perfect pest."

"I am?" he shrieked, batting his eyelashes and pretending to be really happy. "Oh, thank you! Thank you!"

Chapter 13

The rest of the afternoon felt like it was taking forever, but finally, it was three o'clock and time to go home.

Nana picked me up and brought malted milk balls for a treat! Even though I had to go to gymnastics class, she said I could take a few minutes to help Noah talk with J.J. I knew our talk would be quick because Cora had to go to Hebrew school.

"Just-a don' break-a any donkeys!" Nana said, and winked.

I saw Cora and Noah talking to J.J. near the

climbing wall, and very quietly, I ran over and hid around the corner where they couldn't see me.

Guess who was already there, leaning against the wall?

Ivy! Wearing purple lipstick!

"What are you doing here?" I whispered.

"Just making sure everything's A-okay," she said.

"Me, too," I said. I flattened my back against the wall next to her and leaned over as far as I could to hear what they were saying. But then guess who walked over and started talking REALLY LOUDLY?

"What are you guys doing?" Jude asked. Except it sounded like: "WHAT ARE YOU GUYS DOING?"

"Shhhhh!" I whispered. "We're Noah's

backup!" I pointed to Noah and Cora and J.J. around the corner.

Jude and Ezra flattened their backs against the wall next to me and Ivy. "Then we're the backup to the backup," Jude whispered.

The thing about brothers is that even though they can be super annoying, they are always there to help when you need them.

Sticks and Stones

I strained my ears to hear what J.J. was saying. He sounded upset. "But I was just kidding!"

Then came Noah's voice: "Well, it's not funny."

Then came Cora's voice: "How would you like it if Noah made fun of your orange jacket? Or for being really tall? Or for your name? What's J.J. stand for, anyway?"

J.J. didn't say anything.

Noah said, "I don't like it when you call me Shorty." The more he talked, the louder and stronger his voice got. "I don't want you to say it again."

"Rock on, Noah!" Ivy whispered. She was smiling.

"Okay," said J.J.

"If you tease me anymore, my parents are telling Principal Powell," came Noah's voice. It was strong and sure.

"Don't do that! Please!" J.J. pleaded.

Then came Cora's voice: "J.J., will you agree not to call Noah names?"

"I won't do it again," promised J.J. "I'm sorry."

Noah didn't say anything for a minute. Then I heard him say, "Fine."

"Do you want to play soccer?" asked J.J. "Or we could play with my pogo stick—"

Pogo stick! That was the code word! At least I was pretty sure it was. Quick as a flash, I jumped out of my hiding spot and raced over to Noah and Cora and J.J.

"DON'T WORRY!" I shouted. "I'M HERE! Your backup has ARRIVED!!"

Jude and Ezra were right behind me. "Your backup's backup has arrived, too," said Ezra. He didn't say it with a whole lot of pep, though.

Ivy came, too. "Hiya," she said. "What's up?"

Noah and Cora and J.J. were looking at me

like I was a kangaroo with three heads. "What are you doing?" Noah whispered.

"I heard the code word!" I whispered back. "Somebody said *pogo stick*!"

"But the code word was *hopscotch*!" whispered Noah. "And J.J. can't say the code word; only I can!"

He had a point.

Jude and Ezra just shook their heads and walked away.

Ivy laughed.

"Oops! Sorry about that!" I said to Noah. I started to back away from them in little tiny steps. But then I had a better idea. I turned to J.J.

"But since I'm here, I have something to say, too," I said.

I took a deep breath.

"It's not okay for you to make fun of my name—"

"Plus," said Ivy, "Ronny's a totally cool nick-name. It's tough and mysterious."

I was so flattered!

"Why, thank you," I said to Ivy. Then I turned back to J.J.

"And it's not okay to make fun of my clothes, either. I like these jeans. In fact, I don't just like them. I LOVE them. If these jeans were a person,

Sticks and Stones

I might just marry them! I mean, have you *seen* this turquoise glitter star?"

"It's hard-core awesome," Ivy agreed.

"Why, thank you again," I said. And then, to J.J.: "So, I don't care if they're dirty or torn or anything. Don't pick a fight with my pants. *Capisce?*"

Capisce is how Italian people, especially mobsters, say "Understand?"

"Ummm, okay," J.J. said. "I won't fight with your pants."

"Good." I nodded really slowly. "Good."

Then I turned around to find Nana so I could go to gymnastics.

"Hey, nice work," Ivy whispered, giving me a high five. "You're one tough cookie."

As Jude and I put on our backpacks, I saw Noah and J.J. and Ivy kicking the soccer ball around. J.J. looked really happy.

While I was walking out of the yard, I almost bumped into someone walking in. It was the tallest man I've ever seen. He was so tall that I had to bend my neck up, up, up to see his face. And guess what he was wearing on top of his head? An orange hat that said FLORIDA on the front.

Noah was totally right about J.J.'s dad. He was as tall as a redwood tree!

I gulped loudly and waited for Mr. Taylor to yell or tell me to watch where I was going. But he didn't. He just patted me on the head and said, "You okay, kiddo?"

I nodded and then I ran out the gate. Now *that's* what I call enough excitement for one day!

Chapter 14

The next day was Friday. As I like to say: TGIF! I didn't used to know what that meant. Then Jude told me it meant "Tarantulas Gobble Ink Fast!" Which I always thought was a very weird thing for people to say. Then one day, Dad told me that it really meant "Thank Goodness It's Friday!" which made a lot more sense. I am still trying to think of a way to get back at Jude for tricking me. It's on my to-do list.

It was a great day at school, except for the part where Miss Mabel said we were going to do meditation again. Quick as a flash, I raised my hand and asked to go to the bathroom. Then I took a long time washing my hands, and I dragged my feet really, really, really slowly walking back. So I missed the whole meditation! What a relief. Nothing stresses me out more than relaxing!

After school, J.J. ran up to me.

"Here," he said, and he shoved a folded-up piece of paper in my hand. It was written in orange marker, and this is what it said:

> I'm sorry for making fun of your name and your clothes. I was trying to make you laugh.
>
> And by the way, Uncle Ronny is my favorite uncle. He can burp the whole alphabet. Yours truly,
> Jeremiah Jehoshaphat
> p.s. That is what J.J. stands for.
> p.p.s. Don't you dare laugh!

J.J. was watching me read it, so I tried really, really hard not to laugh. I thought of really sad things like ice cream falling off the cone before you have a chance to lick it and baby bunnies who have the flu and get thermometers stuck in their mouths. But then I thought of the name "Jehoshaphat," and I couldn't help it—the corners of my mouth went up in a smile.

"You're going to laugh!" exclaimed J.J.

"No, I'm not!"

"Yes, you are! Your face looks all crazy trying to hold in your laugh. Like this." J.J. made a silly face that looked a lot like Jude's Tough Guy Face or, as I like to call it, the On-the-Toilet Face.

When I saw his face, I couldn't help it. I burst out laughing so hard, I snorted. That made J.J. laugh, too.

When we finally stopped giggling, I said, "It's not the *worst* name I've ever heard."

"Really?" he said hopefully. "What's the worst name you ever heard?"

I thought of Jude's middle name. But I was sworn to secrecy. So I just said, "Top-secret stuff. I could tell you, but then I'd have to kill you."

Noah ran over, with Cora and Camille behind him. The front of Camille's hair looked strange. It was hanging down instead of sticking up like usual. It seemed longer than the rest of her hair. And less curly.

"Hey! Did you put rocks in your hair again?" I asked.

"Yep, because she begged and begged me," said Camille grumpily. "And guess who has a sore neck now?"

But Cora was smiling from ear to ear.

"My makeover worked!" squeaked Cora. "I'm

collecting more rocks so I can do the rest of her hair."

"Never," grumbled Camille.

"Tonight!" squeaked Cora.

"Who wants to play tag?" Noah asked.

"Me!" I said.

"Me, too!" said J.J.

Ivy walked up then and tossed her backpack to the ground. I couldn't believe my eyes. The green chunk of hair wasn't green anymore. It was blue, almost the same color as the star on my knee!

"Count me in," Ivy said.

"Yippee-ki-yay!" I hollered. I'd never played tag with a teenager before, and I'd definitely never played with a teenager who had blue hair!

"What kind of tag should we play?" Cora asked.

"Ooooh, I know!" I said. I got into my crane pose and yelled, "KUNG FU TAG!!!!"

"Well, in that case," said Ivy, "prepare for certain doom. Because I'm IT!"

Then Ivy did the most amazing thing. She got into a perfect crane pose and did a perfect crane kick, with absolutely no falling down.

Ivy knew kung fu? The whole time? She really was a mystery.

I reminded myself to ask her all about it . . . as soon as tag was over.

Take the Fix-It Friends Pledge!

I, (say your full name), do solemnly vow to help kids with their problems. I promise to be kind with my words and actions. I will try to help very annoying brothers even though they probably won't ever need help because they're soooooo perfect. Cross my heart, hope to cry, eat a gross old garbage fly.

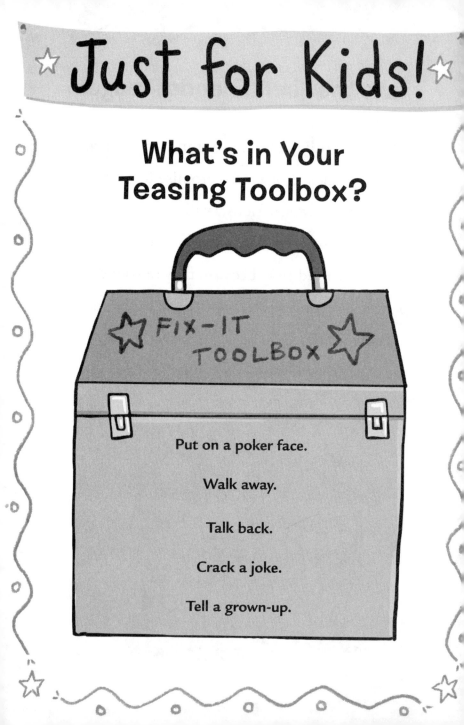

Just for Kids!

What's in Your Teasing Toolbox?

FIX-IT TOOLBOX

Put on a poker face.

Walk away.

Talk back.

Crack a joke.

Tell a grown-up.

When Teasing Ticks You Off . . .

Want to hear something surprising? Everybody gets teased. Ask your mom and your cousin and your next-door neighbor, and they'll remember a time when someone made fun of them. Yep, *everybody* gets teased, and *nobody* likes it.

How does it feel when you get teased?

"I feel like I want to punch them."
—Turtle, age eight

"I feel like I'm the only one being teased."
—Gavin, age twelve

"Some kids don't care if they get teased. But it bothers me that people want to be mean. I don't want to be mean."
—Hannah, age eight

"When I'm playing with someone, it feels like there is a door wide open in between us. But when they say something mean, the door closes a little, and if they're really mean, the door closes all the way."

—Stella, age eight

What did you do that helped stop the teasing?

"I just ignored them and went off to play with my other friends. Don't tease back or fight back, because you might get in trouble instead of them getting in trouble."

—Hadley, age eight

"First say, 'Stop.' If they don't stop, say, 'Buzz off.'"

—Nora, age eight

"One day, a child called me strange and stupid, and I responded, 'Thanks for the compliment.' He just walked away. It helps sometimes to have the opposite reaction they expect you to have because you're not giving them what they want."

—Giovanni, age ten

"The worst thing you can do is not tell an adult. Once you tell somebody, it makes the situation a lot better."

—Edie, age ten

What to Do When You Get Teased

Getting teased can make you feel like you don't have much control, and that can be upsetting. But here's the thing: You *can* control one really important thing. You can control how you respond to the teasing, and that can make all the difference!

It all boils down to three words: *Keep your cool.* Most kids tease to get a big reaction from you. If you yell or tease back or burst into tears, that's exactly the kind of reaction they want, and they'll probably keep right on teasing you. Want to take the target off your back? Keep calm, and act like you just don't care! Here's how:

1. Use your poker face.

You may be steaming mad or really sad—and you should definitely tell a grown-up all about these feelings later. But when you're being teased, don't show the teaser how upset you are. Make your face blank and peaceful, just like *Mona Lisa*.

2. Walk away.

Don't storm off, or the teaser may want to follow. Just act like you have way more interesting stuff to do, and walk away to find other friends you can play with.

3. Be smart about talking back.

If you can't stay silent or just don't

want to, that's okay! You can absolutely stand up for yourself. The key is to stay calm and in control. Try one of these comebacks; they really work!

*Tell them to stop in a firm, confident way:

"What you're doing is not okay" or "Stop it. I'm not going to play with you if you're not nice."

*Act like the teasing is super boring:

"I don't have time for this" or "Tell me something I don't know."

*Surprise them by acting like the teasing doesn't bother you:

"Thanks for the compliment!" or "I'm so glad you noticed!"

4. Ask an adult for help.

If you ever feel unsafe or if a group of kids is ganging up on you, you should get a grown-up right away. And if you've tried to handle the teasing on your own but it continues, ask an adult for help. Teasing is not okay, and you don't have to stand for it.

5. Don't believe the teasing.

Just because someone says something does not make it true. Don't let yourself believe mean comments from teasers! Instead, as a famous singer once said: Shake it off! Talk to people who really know you; they'll remind you how much they care and how special you are. Because you are

awesome, just the way you are!

Want more tips or fixes for other problems?
Just want to check out some Fix-It Friends games
and activities? Go to fixitfriendsbooks.com.

Resources for Parents

If your child is being bullied, here are some resources that may be helpful.

Books for Kids

The Juice Box Bully: Empowering Kids to Stand Up for Others by Bob Sornson and Maria Dismondy, Ferne Press, 2010

A Smart Girl's Guide to Knowing What to Say by Patti Kelley Criswell, American Girl, 2012

Stand Up for Yourself & Your Friends: Dealing with Bullies and Bossiness, and Finding a Better Way by Patti Kelley Criswell, American Girl, 2011

Weird! A Story About Dealing with Bullying in Schools by Erin Frankel, Free Spirit Publishing, 2012

Books for Parents

Best Friends, Worst Enemies: Understanding the Social Lives of Children by Michael Thompson, PhD, and

Catherine O'Neill Grace with Lawrence J. Cohen, PhD, Ballantine, 2001

The Bully, the Bullied, and the Bystander: From Preschool to High School—How Parents and Teachers Can Help Break the Cycle of Violence by Barbara Coloroso, William Morrow, 2009

Websites

Stop Bullying

www.stopbullying.gov/kids

Pacer Center's Kids Against Bullying

www.pacerkidsagainstbullying.org/kab

Pacer's National Bullying Prevention Center

www.pacer.org/bullying

Don't miss the next adventure of

The Fix-It Friends

The Show
Must Go On!

About the Author

Nicole C. Kear grew up in New York City, where she still lives with her husband, three firecracker kids, and a ridiculously fluffy hamster. She's written lots of essays and a memoir, *Now I See You*, for grown-ups, and she's thrilled to be writing for kids, who make her think hard and laugh harder. She has a bunch of fancy, boring diplomas and one red clown nose from circus school. Seriously.

nicolekear.com